# No School for Ben
## What Will Happen?

Daphne Pang

Illustrated by
Dwain Esper

AuthorHouse™
1663 Liberty Drive
Bloomington, IN 47403
www.authorhouse.com
Phone: 833-262-8899

Because of the dynamic nature of the Internet, any web addresses or links contained in this book may have changed since publication and may no longer be valid. The views expressed in this work are solely those of the author and do not necessarily reflect the views of the publisher, and the publisher hereby disclaims any responsibility for them.

Any people depicted in stock imagery provided by Getty Images are models, and such images are being used for illustrative purposes only.
Certain stock imagery © Getty Images.

This book is printed on acid-free paper.

ISBN: 978-1-4918-3321-6 (sc)
ISBN: 978-1-4918-3322-3 (e)

Library of Congress Control Number: 2013920395

Print information available on the last page.

Published by AuthorHouse

Rev. Date: 10/20/2021

authorHOUSE®

# No School for Ben

## What Will Happen?

Ben is a little six year old boy. He lives with his Dad and Mom. Their house is at a corner of two streets in a neighborhood of houses that look like Ben's. He has a lot of fun playing with his friends outside his house every day.

Each early morning, he dresses up to go to school. At the same time, Dad and Mom get ready to go to work. Before he leaves, Ben eats the cereal and milk that Mom brings out for him so he will not be hungry.

He then walks down the driveway to join three other kids to wait for the yellow bus for school. Every day, Ed, the bus driver drives up with the bus at the exact time at the same spot, whether it is in the dark, light, heat, cold, rain or snow.

At school, Christine, the teacher waits for Ben and his classmates to arrive. She teaches them to read, write and count with the same alphabets and numbers until afternoon. Ed then drives Ben home to be with babysitter, Mary, till Dad and Mom comes home. For a long time, Ben does these same things with the same people every day.

One cold Monday morning after a fun weekend, Ben feels sleepy and comfortable under the cover in his warm soft bed. He curls up tighter when he hears Mom's footsteps coming towards his room.

"Ben," whispers Mom from the doorway. "it is time to wake up."

"I do not want to go to school anymore!" Ben murmurs into his pillow and continues to lay in bed.

"Why not?" she asks. Mom walks into his room. She places her hands on his forehead to check for any fever. He is not sick and she sits on his bedside.

"There is no need to go to school any more. I already know all the abc's and numbers. It is the same things to do every day." says Ben as he turns around to face her..

"So, you must be very smart then; enough to help other people by going to school today," replies Mom.

"How can I be of help to anyone.. by going to school?" asks Ben curiously.

"Well," says Mom. "Just imagine. If you, and your friends who follow you, do not go to school, Ed's school bus will be empty. He will soon no longer has a job to come round anymore, to take you to meet your classmates and teacher."

"Hmm.." thought Ben, feeling sad for Ed.

Mom continues, "There will be more new things to learn. But your teacher Christine will not have to be at school because she does not have anyone to teach in the empty classroom. And there will no longer be a school."

"Oh dear," Ben frowns, thinking of teacher Christine whom he likes.

Mom went on, "So you will be at home, not at school. Parents like Dad and I have to watch you at home and earn less money to buy food and clothes."

Soon, the stores will close because us, parents, are not shopping. Every one will be unhappy. You are very important to us all." She added.

Mom looks at her wrist watch and said, "Oh my, look at the time! Every one is waiting for you, at wherever they are. They want to do the same things with you. So, can you help us?" "Okay, Mom!" says Ben proudly.

"Well hurry before Ed drives off!" Mom said.
Ben hops out of bed. "I will help. I want to make you and Dad, Ed, and my teacher Christine happy!"

"Yeah, Ben to the rescue!" says Dad. Ben rushes pass him to brush his teeth, dresses up, then to the kitchen for his cereal, and ride on Ed's bus to school.

Ben is eager to get to school because everybody needs him!